For Dad
—C. F.

For Andy, Caroline, and Charlotte
—J. C.

Margaret K. McElderry Books
An imprint of Simon & Schuster Children's Publishing Division
1230 Avenue of the Americas, New York, New York 10020
Text copyright © 2004 by Claire Freedman
Illustrations copyright © 2004 by Jane Chapman
Published by arrangement with Little Tiger Press,
an imprint of Magi Publications
The text for this book is set in Souvenir.
The illustrations for this book are rendered in acrylic paint.
Manufactured in China
2 4 6 8 10 9 7 5 3 1
Library of Congress Cataloging-in-Publication Data
Freedman, Claire.
Dilly Duckling / Claire Freedman ; illustrated by Jane Chapman.—1st U.S. ed.
p. cm.
Summary: A silly duckling sees one of her feathers fall out and chases after it, only to
learn that she will lose all of her downy feathers before her grown-up feathers appear.
ISBN 0-689-86772-7
[1. Ducks—Fiction. 2. Porcupines—Fiction. 3. Mice—Fiction.] I. Chapman, Jane,
1970- ill. II. Title. PZ7.F87275 Di 2004
[E]—dc22
2003013501

Dilly Duckling

by Claire Freedman

illustrated by Jane Chapman

Margaret K. McElderry Books

New York   London   Toronto   Sydney   Singapore

One sunshiny day the Ducks set off for a family waddle. Little Dilly was last in the line.

"Peekaboo!" Dilly said to the fish.
"Hello!" she called to the bugs
and dragonflies.

"Keep up, Dilly!" Mama Duck
called out.
    But Dilly was busy watching
a big blue butterfly.

She was waddling after it, when suddenly—*puff!*—a gust of wind blew out one of her downy feathers. "Oh, no!" gasped Dilly. "My feather! It's flying away!"

Dilly raced after the fluffy feather.

"Stop that feather!" she quacked loudly.

Wheeee!

The wind blew Dilly's downy feather this way
and that way . . . up in the air . . . and down again.

Around and around in circles Dilly ran dizzily, trying to catch it.

"Come back!" she
called to her feather.
But it floated farther
and farther away.

Dilly flopped to the ground in a daze.

"What am I going to do?" she cried.

"Do about what?" asked Spike.

"My feather," Dilly said with a sigh. "It blew away."

"Was it yellow and fluffy?" Spike asked.

"Yes!" cried Dilly excitedly.

"It drifted down the hill," Spike said.

"I'll get it!"

Spike curled himself into a tight ball.
He rolled downhill, spinning faster and faster.
"I'll try to spear your feather on my spikes!" he
shouted as he whizzed by.

"Wheeeeee!" Spike cried.
"Hooray!" quacked Dilly excitedly.

Bump! Spike landed in a hedge.
Puff! Up flew Dilly's feather again.
Slowly Dilly's feather drifted down,
down, down until it landed in a field.

Dilly and Spike pitter-pattered after it.

"It's caught on a cornstalk," squeaked Nibble. "I'll get it for you!"

"Careful," whispered Dilly. "It's a very important feather!"

Nibble held her breath as she crept through the tall grass. Slowly she climbed the cornstalk. Gently she stretched out her paw. . . .

"Atchoo!" sneezed Nibble as the feather tickled her twitchy nose. *Wheeee!* Off Dilly's feather flew.

The wind blew Dilly's feather up, up in the sky and far, far away.

"Sorry, Dilly!" Nibble called. "It's gone!"

"Oh, no!" quacked Dilly, and she burst into tears.

"Oh, poor Dilly," said Spike.
"Don't cry."
Nibble and Spike gave little
Dilly a cheer-up hug.

"I'll never see my fluffy feather again,"
Dilly said sadly. "I'm going home to tell my
mama."

Dilly waved good-bye to her friends.
"Thank you for trying to help me," she called.

"Mama," Dilly quacked. "One of my big fluffy feathers has fallen out! It's lost forever!"

"Silly Dilly," Mama Duck said, giving Dilly a big cuddle. "*All* your downy feathers will fall out. Then you'll grow new grown-up feathers—just like mine!"

"Really?" quacked Dilly in surprise. "So I'll look just like you!"

Dilly and Mama Duck joined the ducklings splashing in the river.

"Look!" Dilly cried. "There's my feather!"

"So it is," said Mama Duck.

"I don't need it anymore, do I?" Dilly giggled. "I'll grow another one!"

And quacking happily, she dilly-dallied off to play.